JACK RUSSELL: Dog Detective

The Awful Pawful

P9-AQD-231

DARREL & SALLY ODGERS

SCHOLASTIC CANADA LTD.

New York   Toronto   London   Auckland   Sydney
Mexico City   New Delhi   Hong Kong   Buenos Aires

Scholastic Canada Ltd.
604 King Street West, Toronto, Ontario M5V 1E1, Canada

Scholastic Inc.
557 Broadway, New York, NY 10012, USA

Scholastic Australia Pty Limited
PO Box 579, Gosford, NSW 2250, Australia

Scholastic New Zealand Limited
Private Bag 94407, Greenmount, Auckland, New Zealand

Scholastic Children's Books
Euston House, 24 Eversholt Street, London NW1 1DB, UK

Library and Archives Canada Cataloguing in Publication
Odgers, Darrel
The awful pawful / Darrel & Sally Odgers ; illustrations by Janine Dawson.
(Jack Russell, dog detective ; #5)
ISBN 978-0-439-93798-6

I. Odgers, Sally, 1957-   II. Dawson, Janine   III. Title.
IV. Series: Odgers, Darrel   Jack Russell, dog detective ; #5.
PZ7.O2374Aw 2007   j823'.92   C2006-906733-3

First published by Scholastic Press in 2006.
Text copyright © 2006 by Sally and Darrel Odgers.
Cover design copyright © 2006 Lake Shore Graphics.
Dog, Frisbee, courtesy of the Cansick family.
Interior illustrations by Janine Dawson.
Interior illustrations copyright © 2006 Scholastic Australia.

6 5 4 3 2 1   Printed in Canada   07 08 09 10 11

Dear Readers,

The story you're about to
read is about me and my
friends and how we solved
the Case of the Awful Pawful. To save
time, I'll introduce us all to you now.
Of course, if you know us already, you
can trot off to Chapter One.

I am Jack Russell, Dog Detective.
I live with my landlord, Sarge, in
Doggeroo. Sarge detects human-type
crimes. I have the important job of
detecting crimes that deal with dogs.
I'm a Jack Russell terrier, so I am
dogged and intelligent.

Auntie Tidge and Foxy live next door
to Sarge and me. Auntie Tidge is lovely.
She has dog biscuits. Foxy is not lovely.
He's a fox terrier (more or less). He used

1

to be a street dog and a thief, but he's reformed now. Auntie Tidge has even gotten rid of his fleas. Foxy sometimes helps me with my cases.

Uptown Lord Setter (Lord Red for short) lives in Uptown House with Caterina Smith. Lord Red means well, but he isn't very bright.

We have other friends in Doggeroo. These include Polly the dachshund, Jill Russell, the squekes, and Shuffle the pug. Then there's Fat Molly Cat from the library.

That's all you need to know, so let's start with Chapter One.

Yours doggedly,

Jack Russell—the detective with a nose for crime

DogLess Doggeroo

We had been on vacation with Sarge
and Auntie Tidge, but Foxy and I were
glad when the train arrived at the
station. Vacations are fun, but there's
no place like home.

Jack Johnson, the stationmaster,
patted me. "Welcome back, Jack! You
take care of that handsome nose!"

I hoped Jill Russell, who lives at
the station, had heard that.

I shook the train noise out of my
ears. I **sneefled** the train smell out of
my nose. Then I made a quick **nose
map**.

Jack's Map

1. Nest of birds in a tree.

2. Crumbs on bird feeder.

3. Cat.

4. Flowers.

5. Chickens in coops.

6. Rabbits in burrows.

"That's odd," I said to Foxy.

"What is?" Foxy sat down to scratch his belly. (Auntie Tidge wouldn't let him scratch on the train.)

Foxy is my pal, but he doesn't think like a detective.

"What can you smell?" I asked.

Foxy *sniff-sniffed*. "Birds, crumbs, cat, chickens, and rabbits." He started to drool. "I'm hungry, Jack."

"You're always hungry," I said. "What *can't* you smell?"

"Beef bones," said Foxy. "**Special biscuits**. Sausages. Cheese. Dog treats."

I growled. "You can't smell *dog*, Foxy," I said.

"How do you know what I can't smell?" Foxy asked.

Jack's Facts

*Jack Russell terriers have the keenest
noses of all.*
*If a Jack Russell can't smell something,
it can't be smelled.*
Especially not by a fox terrier.
This is a fact.

"Jill Russell lives here. Can you
smell Jill Russell today?"

Foxy *sniff-sniffed*. "No. Maybe she
doesn't want to see you."

Dogwash! Jill Russell always wants
to see me. She pokes me with her nose.
That proves how much she likes me.

I set my nose to super-sniffer mode.

I *sniff-sniffed* left and right. I *sniff-
sniffed* back and forth. No Jill Russell.

On our way home, we passed
Shuffle the pug's house. There was not
a whiff of Shuffle, either. We passed
Ralf Boxer's house. I *sniff-sniffed* there.
There was not a whiff of Ralf Boxer.
I failed to smell Polly Smote or the
three squekes on the corner.

Had all the dogs of Doggeroo been
dognapped while we were away?

This was a case for a detective with a nose for crime.

Jack's Glossary

Sneefle. *A snorting sneeze, done to clear the nose.*

Nose map. *Way of storing information collected by the nose.*

Special biscuits. *Auntie Tidge makes these. They don't harm terrier teeth.*

Dogwash. *Nonsense.*

Dognapped. *Kidnapping done to a dog.*

 # The Awful Pawful

"We must investigate, Foxy," I said.

Foxy said he wanted dinner first.

"After dinner the scent will be cold," I reminded him.

Foxy's belly rumbled. "The scent is already cold," he pointed out. "This dognapping could have happened at any time since we left."

Foxy went to tell Auntie Tidge about dinner.

Jack's Facts

People don't speak Dog.
Dogs don't speak Person.
You don't have to speak the same
language to talk about dinner.
This is a fact.

I got into my basket and chewed my **squeaker bone** while I assessed the situation. Jack Russell's the name, detection's the game!

Detection starts with deduction.

1. Doggeroo seemed dogless, except for Foxy and me.
2. Jill Russell wasn't at the station. Jack Johnson was at the station. That meant he hadn't taken

Jill Russell on vacation.

3. Jack Johnson had told me to take care of my handsome nose. Was someone dognapping dogs with handsome noses?

No. Shuffle the pug was missing. Shuffle does not have a handsome nose.

I bit my squeaker bone harder.

"Jack! Jack!"

Lord Red pranced along the street like a hairy whirlwind. I deduced there were still *some* dogs in Doggeroo.

"Jack? Jack, are you hooooome?" Lord Red peered over my gate. "Jack? I'm **pawfully** glad to see you, Jack. I've been so looooonely!"

"Does Caterina Smith know you're out?" I asked.

Lord Red looked surprised. "She is away. Can I enter your **terrier-tory**?"

Jack's Facts

Polite dogs ask **pawmission** _before they enter another dog's terrier-tory. Red is a polite dog. Politeness has nothing to do with brains. This is a fact._

I gave pawmission, and Lord Red sailed over my gate. He pranced to my porch. "I'm glad to see you, Jack," he said. "I've been so looooonely since the Awful Pawful came to Doggeroo."

"The *what?*"

"Caterina Smith makes me stay in the yard. I really . . ."

"Red!" I said.

". . . missed you and Foxy and . . ." said Red.

"Stop, in the name of the paw!" I yapped.

Red sat down. "Yes, Jack?"

I stared at him. "Explain properly."

"Caterina Smith won't . . ."

"*Red!*"

Red borrowed my squeaker bone. I stared. Red is a polite dog, and polite dogs do not borrow another dog's treasures without pawmission. If Red had forgotten his manners, something serious had happened. That's why I didn't give him a sharp reminder.

"What has come to Doggeroo?"
I demanded.

"The Awful Pawful."

"What's an Awful Pawful?"

Red put his paw on my squeaker
bone. "Nobody knows. It has an awful
pawful of claws. It leaves dogs' noses
sore and bleeding."

"Your nose looks fine," I said.

Lord Red crossed his eyes to see
his nose. "The Awful Pawful can't get
me. Caterina Smith says I'm safe in
my special yard when she isn't home."

"Why don't you get a **dog door**?"
I asked. Sarge made special dog doors

for Foxy and me before we went away.

Red shuddered. "I hate dog doors,
Jack. I ouched my tail in one once.
I don't need a dog door. If Caterina
Smith is away, I stay safe in my
special yard." He chewed my squeaker
bone again. He was really rattled.

"You're not in your special yard,"
I reminded him.

Red crunched down hard. The
squeaker bone squawked. "I'm not
safe! The Awful Pawful will get
meeee!" He sprang off the porch, sailed
over the gate, and howled off home.

I put my paw on my squeaker
bone. It smelled of Lord Red, so I
rolled on it so it would smell like me
again. As I jumped up, Foxy crawled
through the gap between his house

and mine. "What was *that* about?"

"An Awful Pawful has been attacking dogs' noses."

"Is that why the dogs are missing?" Foxy asked. "Are they all at the vet's?" The whites of his eyes showed. Foxy knows what happens to dogs at the vet's. Needles. Pills. Things stuck under your tail.

"If Jill Russell was at the vet's, her person would be with her," I said.

"Maybe he left her there to have her nose sewn up," said Foxy.

That upset me. How could Jill Russell poke me with her nose if it was sewn up? I chewed my squeaker bone for comfort and discovered something **terrier-able**. My squeaker bone had lost its squeak.

Jack's Glossary

Squeaker bone. *Item for exercising teeth. Not to be confused with a toy.*

Pawfully. *Very, awfully.*

Terrier-tory. *A territory owned by a terrier.*

Pawmission. *Permission, given by a dog.*

Dog door. *A door for dogs.*

Terrier-able. *Very bad.*

Mark of the Awful Pawful

I buried my squeaker bone under my blanket. I felt as if I had lost a friend, but it was my own fault. I should never have let Red touch it. I would tell him so later, but right now I had a case to solve.

"What do you do when you are hurt, Foxy?" I asked.

"I yelp," said Foxy. "Then I go through my dog door to get a special biscuit from Auntie Tidge."

I was hungry and upset. I wanted a special biscuit myself. Instead, I

pawsisted. "What do you do next?"

"I hide under Auntie Tidge's bed."

Jack's Facts

*People think beds are for people to
sleep in.*
*Dogs think beds are for dogs to hide
under.*
Dogs know better than people.
This is a fact.

It was time to check under some
beds.

Foxy went home. I left the yard
(never mind how) and set off.

The three squekes live with Dora
Barkins, not far from Auntie Tidge.
You never see a squeke on its own.

They work as a team and are always yipping in packs. Today, their yard was empty.

I **Jack-jumped** over their gate and trotted around.

No squekes.

I sniffed busily in the corners of the yard.

No squekes.

I chased sparrows. I found three bones the squekes had buried and dug them up.

Still no squekes.

I sniffed under Dora Barkins's door and made a nose map.

Jack's Map

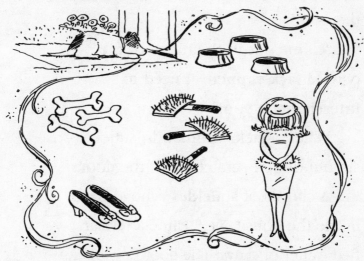

1. Three bowls.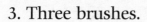

2. Three rubber bones.

3. Three brushes.

4. A pair of shoes.

5. Dora Barkins.

But, no—yes! I detected a trace of the squekes.

"Come out in the name of the paw!" I **Jack-yapped**. "I need to **interrier-gate** you!"

When a Jack commands, squekes should obey. I scratched on the door.

A chorus of **squekles** echoed from inside the house. Next came a **terrier-fied** clatter of claws. The door flew open.

SPLOSH!

That was a bucket of cold water hitting me. I gasped and spluttered.

"Get away, you brute! Go on, get!"

That was Dora Barkins yelling at me.

"Jack? Jack Russell? What the—"

That was Dora Barkins recognizing me. But she was a bucketful of water too late.

I shot past Dora Barkins and zipped through the house. I *drip-sniff-sniffed* under every door as I ran.

Even a soaking can't distract a tracking Jack. The squekes were hiding under a bed in the fourth room I searched. I crawled in after them.

Squekling wildly, the squekes shot out the other side. They jammed themselves in a corner and tried to dig through the wall. "Ow-ow-ow!" they panicked. "*Awful clawful pawful . . .*"

"Stop that!" I Jack-yapped. I gave the nearest squeke a push with my nose. It cowered. The others hid under their long hair and quivered.

Before I could interrier-gate them, Dora Barkins came in. The squekes hurled themselves at her knees. She gathered them up in her arms. "It's all right, boys." Then she spotted me. "Jack, go home! I have to take the boys to the vet's."

I went. I had seen enough. On the nose of every squeke were ten red bleeding marks, left by the Awful Pawful.

Jack's Glossary

Pawsisted. *Kept doggedly on.*

Jack-jump. *A sudden spring made by a Jack Russell terrier.*

Jack-yap. *A loud, piercing yap made by a Jack Russell terrier.*

Interrier-gate. *Official questioning, done by a terrier.*

Squekle. *The rare sound of a terrified squeke.*

Terrier-fied. *Frightened by a terrier; also a frightened terrier.*

25

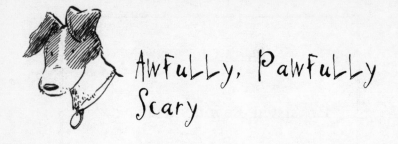

Awfully, Pawfully Scary

I paused to consider what I knew.

The squekes were scared enough to hide. It takes something really scary to scare a squeke. The Awful Pawful must be really, *really* scary.

I was wet and cold. I wanted to go straight home, but I still had work to do. Doggedly, I set off to see if Shuffle and Polly were hiding in their houses. If Shuffle and Polly had met the Awful Pawful, I could interrier-gate them and get a description.

I went to Shuffle's back door and

sniffed hard. I could smell Shuffle in there. I also smelled something else.

Jack's Facts

All dogs do what dogs have to do.
Clean dogs don't do it in the house
unless they are too scared to go out.
Shuffle is a clean dog.
Shuffle had done it in the house.
Therefore, Shuffle was too scared to go
out.
This is a fact.

"Shuffle?" I scratched the door.

I listened. I heard a faint snuffle.

"Come out, Shuffle," I Jack-yapped.

"I'm shut in," said Shuffle.

"I'll bark for backup. Sarge will

make you a special dog door."

"I don't *want* a dog door," wheezed Shuffle. "Go home, Jack. Save your nose!"

I was right. Shuffle was scared. He had met the Awful Pawful.

"Describe the Awful Pawful," I pawsisted.

Shuffle whined. "It's a . . . I didn't see it. It hurt my nose a lot. Go away!"

"Shuffle, your nose is evidence. I could arrest you for withholding evidence."

"My nose is shut in with me," Shuffle reminded me.

I Jack-jumped to examine the evidence through the window.

Shuffle's nose always looked terrier-able, but today it looked terrier-ably terrier-able.

"The Awful Pawful hurt your nose," I said. "That means you must have seen the criminal."

"I didn't! I didn't!" Shuffle panicked. "I'm going under the bed now, Jack."

"Stop!" I said. I'm in your **territory** without pawmission!"

"I don't care!" said Shuffle.

I was shocked.

My next witness was Polly Smote. I didn't expect Polly to be **daching** around in her yard. I was right.

Gloria Smote was on her porch with Jill Russell's person, Jack Johnson. I sneaked up behind them.

"It's worth a try," said Jack Johnson.

"Anything's worth a try," said Gloria Smote. "Polly won't go out. She even . . ." Gloria Smote dropped her voice, but Jacks have sharp ears. "She even did her business in the hall."

"So did Jill," said Jack Johnson.

"Ranger Jack *must* deal with this!" said Gloria Smote.

Ranger Jack catches dogs who do bad things and puts them in the pound.

I sneaked into the hall behind Gloria Smote. It smelled of disinfectant. **Ig-gnawing** that, I tracked down Polly, hiding under Gloria Smote's bed.

"Show me your nose."

"I will not!" Polly put both front paws over her nose and yelped. "Get out, Jack Russell."

"Now, Polly," I said. "I know you're ashamed, but—"

"Why should I be ashamed?" snapped Polly.

I didn't remind Polly of what she did in the hall. I changed the subject. "Why is Jill Russell's person here?"

"He's talking about dog doors with Gloria Smote," moaned Polly.

"**Pawfect**!" I said. "You can go in and out whenever you want."

"Yes, and so can the monster ca—" Polly broke off. "Out, Jack Russell!"

"I haven't finished my in-terrier-gation," I said.

Polly snapped at my nose. I backed away. "I'm going, I'm going!"

"Make sure you do!" Polly

retreated. I had seen enough. On her long dachshund nose were ten deep marks left by the Awful Pawful.

This was getting awfully, pawfully scary.

Jack's Glossary

Territory. *A terrier-tory owned by a dog that is not a terrier.*

Daching. *The way dachshunds get around.*

Ig-gnaw. *Ignore, done by dogs.*

Pawfect. *Perfect, for dogs. For cats it would be purrfect.*

Brain Wave

Foxy was on my porch waiting for
me.

"Auntie Tidge went to see Kitty
Booker," he said. "I didn't want to go."

"Maybe you're scared of Fat Molly
Cat?" I teased.

Foxy hackled. "Dogwash! It's
because Fat Molly calls me bad names
in **catspeak**. And I hate the way she
twitches her tail and flicks her ears.
And she does that thing with her
whiskers.

"It makes me want to chase her

up trees," said Foxy, "but Auntie Tidge won't let me. That's why I don't want to visit Kitty Booker. Did you detect any dognapped dogs?"

"We were barking up the wrong tree," I said. I explained my findings to Foxy. "They're not dognapped. Just hiding from the Awful Pawful."

I pulled my squeaker bone out from under my blanket.

Then I remembered it had been desqueakered by Lord Red.

I gave it a little chew. It didn't squeak. It sighed.

"Jack, *Jack*! Heeelllp! Jack!" Lord Red tore along the street. "Jack, Jack, save meeeeeee!" He sailed over my gate. In two more bounds, he reached the porch. I ig-gnawed him.

"Jack, Jack, the Awful Pawful is
after me! Save meeee!"

"Save yourself," I muttered.

"What's wrong with Jack, Foxy?"
asked Red.

"You desqueakered his squeaker bone," said Foxy.

"I did not! I never did! I wouldn't!"

I bit the squeaker bone. It sighed.

"Um . . . did I?" said Red.

I snarled. "You put your fang right through it."

"I only chewed it. Squeaker bones are meant to be chewed."

"Terrier squeaker bones are not made for setter-size fangs."

"Would you like my ball? Or my teddy bear? Or—"

"No!" I growled. "Just tell me what you know about the Awful Pawful."

Red sat down. "Sure, Jack. The Awful Pawful has an awful pawful of claws. It leaves dogs' noses sore and bleeding."

"Yes?" I said. "And?"

"That's all, Jack."

Lord Red is a dog treat short of a full box. I'd have to do this the hard way.

"Have you ever seen the Awful Pawful, Lord Red?" I asked.

"No," said Red.

"You said it was after you!"

"It's after all the dogs of Doggeroo," said Red, "so it must be after me."

"Has anyone ever seen it?"

"The ones with sore noses must have," said Red. "You can't get your nose hurt without seeing the hurter."

"What if it was dark?" said Foxy. "You might be asleep. You'd have your blanket over your head and your nose sticking out. The Awful Pawful might creep up and fasten its fangs on your snout. You wouldn't see it then."

"It doesn't use fangs," said Red. "It uses an awful pawful of claws."

That's when I had a brain wave. "**Pawhaps** Fat Molly is the Awful Pawful," I said. I listed the evidence against her. "She has claws. She hates dogs. She can get in and out of yards." I was sure I had solved the Case of the Awful Pawful.

Jack's Glossary

Catspeak. *The way cats talk.*

Pawhaps. *Perhaps.*

Clue of the Cat-erwaul

"Dogwash!" said Foxy. "Fat Molly can't be the Awful Pawful. What dog would be so scared of a fat cat like that?"

I saw what he meant, but Fat Molly was my only suspect.

"Foxy," I said, "I need your help."

"No," said Foxy.

"You don't know what I want you to do yet!"

"You are not using me as bait," said Foxy. He climbed off my porch and stalked off home. His dog door banged behind him.

"Red, maybe you . . ."

"Not this time, Jack!"

"I'd keep watch and protect you,"
I said.

"I know!" said Red. "You act as
bait. *I'll* keep watch."

That wouldn't work. Red would
run away, or Caterina Smith would
call him home. I'd get my nose hurt
for nothing.

I explained to Red why he was
better bait than me.

"You're a big dog," I said. "Fat
Molly can't reach your nose with her
paws."

"What if it isn't Fat Molly? What if
it's *big*?"

"You can escape through the
nearest dog door."

"My tail will get ouched!"

"Would you rather have a slightly ouched tail or a terrier-ably hurt nose?"

"Neither," said Red.

"Go through my dog door now," I suggested. "I'll watch your tail."

Red stuck his nose through my dog door, then backed away.

"You can do it!" I said.

I went in and out a few times to show him. "Tuck your tail down."

Red tucked his tail down. It floated up again.

"Caterina Smith is calling," he said. "Goodbye, Jack. I'll use the dog door another time."

He dashed off. I cocked my ears. I couldn't hear Caterina Smith calling.

Jack's Facts

*Jack Russell terriers have the sharpest
ears.
If a Jack Russell can't hear something,
it can't be heard.
Especially not by a red setter with
hairy ears.
This is a fact.*

I slept in my basket for a while. It
was nearly dark when I woke. I was
about to discuss supper with Sarge
when I heard something faintly in the
distance.

Yeeeowww-psssst!

My hackles went up. I'd know that
cat-erwaul anywhere. Fat Molly was
calling someone something terrier-able.

Yeeeowww-psssst!

Suddenly, I was terrier-ably angry. Fat Molly deserved a lesson and I was just the Jack to teach her. I left my yard (never mind how) and tracked the cat-erwaul. I was hot on the trail.

I raced past Foxy's house and the squekes' yard. I galloped over the bridge and turned off toward the library.

Yeeeowww-psssst!

I was playing **Cat-ch Cat**. I knew I'd catch Fat Molly and corner her. I would roll her over with a low tackle and teach her a lesson.

Yeeeowww-psssst! Yeeeowww-wongwongwong-psssst!

As I got closer, Fat Molly's cat-erwaul got louder. It sounded scary.

Er-rowww! Psssssttt! Yeeeechhhh!

I slowed down. Was it wise to go
rushing into trouble? What if Fat
Molly wasn't the Awful Pawful?
Worse, what if she was? Maybe I
should check Fat Molly's claws for bits
of nose.

Fat Molly and Kitty Booker live
behind the library. I decided to
approach with caution.

I was on the library steps when
Molly sprang and landed on my back.
She clutched with her claws. I lost my
balance. We rolled down the steps,
clawing, barking, spitting, and nipping.

Woff! Yeeeowww-psssst! Aghhh!
Zzzt! Yip!

We hit the bottom. Molly was
underneath.

"Fat Molly, I am arresting you—"

Yeeeowww-psssst! Brffft! squawked Fat Molly. She reached up with both front paws and stuck them in my snout.

I yelped. I snarled. I had caught the Awful Pawful **red-pawed**.

Jack's Glossary

Cat-erwaul. *A horrible noise made by a cat.*

Cat-ch Cat. *A game dogs play with cats.*

Red-pawed. *Red-handed, but for dogs or cats. Unable to argue, guilty without a doubt.*

Terrier-Fied

I yelped and licked my nose. It hurt a bit, but it wasn't bleeding.

Fat Molly snarled and struggled, and I snapped at her to keep still.

I wish I could say I was being brave, but I was having doubts. If Fat Molly was the Awful Pawful, why wasn't my nose hurting a *lot*?

"Tell the truth, Fat Molly," I ordered. "Are you, or are you not, the Awful Pawful?"

Yeeeowww-psssst! Brffft!

Nine claws swung up toward my nose.

As I jerked my head out of range, I saw my mistake. Fat Molly had nine claws. She had lost one claw from her right front paw.

I put my right front paw on her shoulder and looked down at her. Fat Molly glared back. Her eyes were slits. Her fangs flashed. Molly's face was a mess. I counted ten bleeding wounds.

Fat Molly was bleeding. Therefore, Fat Molly was *not* the Awful Pawful. She was its victim. That meant the Awful Pawful attacked cats as well as dogs.

Yeeeowww-wongwongwong-psssst! Rowwwwweeeeerrahhh!

My hackles rose again. Something had cat-erwauled on the steps above me. Fat Molly twisted out from under my belly and fled.

I looked up—right into the eyes of the Awful Pawful.

The Awful Pawful was a ginger tomcat. He was twice as big as Fat Molly. He had the kind of fangs that give you nightmares.

Yeeeowww-wongwongwong-psssst!
Rowwwwweeeeerrahhh!

I don't speak cat, but I knew what
he meant. He was saying, "You are a
dog. I am a cat. You have teeth. I have
teeth *and* claws. I am bigger than you.
I eat Jack Russells for breakfast."

That double pawful of awful claws
was terrier-fying.

The tomcat stalked down the
steps. His hackles were bigger than
mine. His tail whipped like a snake.
He lifted one paw. I saw clumps of
white fur on his claws. They were bits
of Molly.

I ran home, passing Fat Molly on
the way.

Yeeeowww-wongwongwong-psssst!
Rowwwwweeeeerrahhh!

The Awful Pawful's yowl followed us. I heard a *sciiiiitch* of claws as Fat Molly shot up a tree in Auntie Tidge's yard.

I panted into my yard. My heart pounded harder than my paws. My tail was tucked under my belly.

I dived through my dog door, dashed through the kitchen, and shot under Sarge's bed.

Sarge came into the room. "Jack? What's up, Jack?"

I cringed. Now I knew why the squekes had tried to burrow through the wall. I knew why Polly, Shuffle, and Jill Russell had been dirty dogs in the house. I knew why everyone wanted to hide under beds.

"Jack! Suppertime."

I heard Sarge banging on my bowl. My bowl was on the front porch, next to my basket. What if the Awful Pawful attacked while I was eating? I had to warn Sarge. And what about Auntie Tidge? I had to warn Foxy, too.

Sarge pulled me out from under the bed. "What have you been up to, Jack? You need some iodine on that nose."

Under the Bed

In the morning, I crept out from under the bed.

"Now then, Jack," I told myself. "You met the Awful Pawful, and you escaped without a bleeding nose. If you can do it once, you can do it again."

At last I crept to the porch to eat last night's dinner. I was too late. Foxy was polishing my bowl, and he didn't even look scared. Of course, he hadn't met the Awful Pawful.

"Hi, Jack. Nice of you to share your food."

I scanned my yard. Cats climb. Cats spring and run up trees. Fences that keep dogs in don't keep cats out.

Cats get in through windows. Cats can use dog doors. Cats can . . .

<u>Jack's Facts</u>

Dogs laugh at cats. Cats hiss at dogs. Dogs chase cats. Cats run and hide. Secretly, dogs are terrier-fied of cats. This is a secret fact.

Foxy was staring at me. "What's that on your nose, Jack?"

"Fat Molly clawed me when I tried to arrest her."

Foxy scratched his belly. "You okay, Jack? You look terrier-able. Did you get any sleep last night?"

"I was thinking about the case," I said.

Foxy scratched his ear.

"Foxy."

"I am not going to be bait," said Foxy.

I shuddered. "Last night, after I tried to arrest Fat Molly, I met the Awful Pawful."

Foxy stopped scratching his ear. "Why didn't you arrest it, then?"

I was about to say I'd been gathering evidence, when a terrier-able sound interrupted me.

Yeeeowww-wongwongwong-psssst! Rowwwwweeeeerrahhh!

It was the Awful Pawful springing onto my gate.

Zoooop! Clonk-onk-onk-ock.

My dog door banged as Foxy and
I dashed into the house. We scuttled
through the kitchen and hid under
Sarge's bed.

"*That's* why I didn't make an
arrest," I said.

Foxy licked his lips nervously. "I
don't blame you," he said.

I told Foxy my conclusions. "The
suspect attacks cats as well as dogs," I

said. "I think he wants Doggeroo for himself. He will do this by terrier-fying everyone. Dogs can't defend their territories when they're hiding under beds."

"I suppose that's it, then," said Foxy. "I'll have to move on. Again."

"Dogwash!" I said. "How does the Awful Pawful get the upper paw on dogs?"

"He claws their noses," said Foxy. "He terrier-fies them."

"That's not all," I said. "The victims won't admit that the Awful Pawful is a *cat*. They are too ashamed. Their shame gives the Awful Pawful his power. Are we going to let him keep that power?"

"Probably," said Foxy.

"We are not!" I was so excited, I Jack-jumped.

<u>Jack's Facts</u>

Jacks often Jack-jump when excited.
Jack-jumping under a bed is a bad idea.
This is a fact.

"What can we do?" asked Foxy.

"We must get the upper paw," I
said. "We must shame the Awful
Pawful."

"Just you and me?" asked Foxy.

"No," I said. "This is a job for the
Jack-pack."

<u>Jack's Glossary</u>

Jack-pack. *A noble pack of
dogs united under a strong
leader.*

Council of Paw

When a Jack Russell commands, dogs obey. But the dogs were scared, and the Awful Pawful was on the prowl. Raising a Jack-pack wouldn't be easy.

I made a lot of nose maps that day. Most of them were like this:

Jack's Map

1. Foxy.

2. The Awful Pawful.

3. Trees without birds.

At last, I made one that was better.

Jack's Map

1. Foxy.

2. The empty street.

3. Birds hopping around
under the trees.

   Quickly, stopping often to make
more nose maps, I went to visit the
squekes. They were still in hiding, so I
had to rally them through their new
dog door.

   "I met the Awful Pawful!" I
announced.

   That set the squekes to squekling
again. "Ow-ow-ow! Awful clawful
pawful . . ."

   "He is a pawfully scary cat," I said.
"I was terrier-fied. I ran away."

Six bulging eyes peered at me.

"I believe he plans to take every territory in Doggeroo," I said. "Can we let that happen?"

A squeke gave a faint yip. "He hurt us a lot."

"Join the Jack-pack," I said. "Not even an Awful Pawful can terrier-fy us then. After all," I added, "I'm sure you three squekes are better than any cat, even a pawfully scary cat like that."

The squekes shuddered.

"Come on," I urged. "It will make the other dogs proud to know the squekes were the first to join the pack."

The squekes liked that. They started yipping agreement.

"My place, tomorrow afternoon," I said. "Make a nose map to make sure it's safe to come."

I trotted off to talk to the other victims. They were scared, too, but dogs have their pride. How could they admit they weren't as brave as a squeke?

The next afternoon, while Sarge was at work, seventeen dogs crowded into my terrier-tory. The **council of paw** had begun.

"The case is solved," I announced. "I need every dog to help with the arrest. We must shame this cat as he has shamed us. We must tree him."

"You can only tree a cat if he's scared," said Jill Russell. She hadn't poked me today. Her nose was too sore. "This cat is scared of no one. What if he hurts us again? My people are away, so there's no one to save me."

"He will be scared of the Jack-pack. And the only thing that will get hurt is the Awful Pawful's pride."

"How is this going to work?" asked Jill Russell.

I explained exactly what everyone was to do. "Go about your business.

The first dog to see, hear, or smell the Awful Pawful must bark for backup."

"We won't all hear that," protested Shuffle.

"At least one of us will," I said firmly. "Whoever hears the first dog must pass the message along by barking that dog's name. Anyone who hears the second dog will do the same thing. That way we'll know where to go. Let's practice now, but quietly. I will take the first turn."

I looked up at my gate and pretended to see the Awful Pawful. "*Backup!*" I barked. "Now, Foxy, you'd be the first to hear me, so what do you need to say?"

"Jack Russell!" yapped Foxy.

"Jack Russell!" yipped the squekes,

and Ralf Boxer and Polly Smote chimed in.

When I was sure everyone knew what to do, I dismissed the Jack-pack. After that, I went about my business. I hoped someone would bark for backup soon.

I was in the kitchen when my dog door banged.

"Jack? Jack? Are you there?" Lord Red was peering at me through the gap.

"What is it?" I demanded. "Has someone barked for back-up?"

"**Of paws** not," said Red. "I came to keep you company. Can I come in?"

"I thought you were afraid of dog doors?" I said.

"I am," said Lord Red, "but I'm even more scared of the Awful Pawful."

"Come in, then," I said.

Lord Red put his front paws through the dog door. "I'm doing it," he said. "I'm using a dog door. I am—"

He was moving a little farther when I heard a distant bark. It sounded like Ralf Boxer.

"Jill Russell!" he was barking. "Jill Russell! Jill Russell!"

As I sprang to attention, I heard the squekes take up the chant. It was time to go.

Jack's Glossary

Council of paw. *A council of war, especially for dogs.*

Of paws. *Of course.*

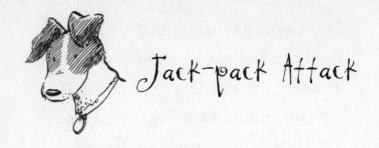

Jack-pack Attack

I bounced to the dog door, but Red
was still halfway through.

"Hurry!" I snapped to Red. "I have
to lead the Jack-pack!"

Red didn't move. "I can't hurry. I
think I'm stuck."

"A Jack-pack can't attack without a
Jack in the lead!" I barked. "Back out!"

"I can't. My tail will get ouched."

"If you don't, your nose will get
ouched, and I'm the Jack to ouch it!" I
yapped.

I could hear Foxy barking now.

"Jill Russell! Jill Russell!"

In my mind, I saw the Jack-Pack forming without me.

A Jack-Pack must have a Jack to lead it, and Jill Russell was alone and in danger. I *had* to get out, *now*.

There was only one thing to do, and so I did it. I got down on my elbows and squirmed under Red's belly, giving his tail a good nip on the way.

Red yelped and shot into the kitchen. I Jack-jumped and hit the porch running. I left the yard and raced out into the street.

"Jill Russell! Jill Russell!" Foxy was still passing on the message as he crawled under his gate. I joined him, and we galloped along the street together.

The Jack-pack was forming quickly as dogs passed the message around Doggeroo. By the time we reached the station there were fifteen of us.

The Awful Pawful was stalking Jill Russell when the Jack-pack swept down the street. Jill was bouncing about bravely, but she was relieved to see us.

"About time!" she yapped.

The Awful Pawful turned and glared at us. For an instant, he flashed his fangs.

I flashed mine back.

The Awful Pawful turned tail and yowled away.

Yeeeowww-wongwongwong-psssst! Rowwwwweeeeerrahhh!

"Jack-pack to the rescue!" I

ordered. "Don't let the Awful Pawful get away!"

The pack closed ranks and galloped across the grassy place that leads to the river.

"Tree that cat!" I barked.

The Awful Pawful had three choices. He could face the pack. He could swim the river. Or he could climb the tree. He chose the tree. That was his mistake.

As he reached the first branch, the Jack-pack formed a ring around the tree.

He stared down and flashed his fangs. We stared up and flashed ours.

He was the biggest cat we had ever seen.

Just then, Lord Red tore up, howling excitedly.

"Jack, Jack! The Awful Pawful
attacked my tail! I'm a victim! I
escaped. I barked for back-up! Your
person let me out of your kitchen! He
is coming. So is Caterina Smith. So
are Dora Barkins, and Tina Boxer,
and—"

Yeeeowww-wongwongwong-psssst!

The Awful Pawful began to
cat-erwaul.

The Jack-pack set up a song of dogged defiance.

That's when our people began to arrive. Sarge came first, with Kitty Booker behind him. Next came Ranger Jack, driving his special van.

"What's going on?" yelled Kitty Booker. "Are those dogs hurting my Molly?"

Sarge pushed through the Jack-pack.

I Jack-jumped into his arms and **greeted** him.

"Foxy Woxy?" That was Auntie Tidge, so Foxy greeted her. Red stopped howling and greeted Caterina Smith. Then he greeted Kitty Booker as well. With all the greetings, the **dog song** died down. Only the Awful Pawful kept yowling.

When I found myself greeting Ranger Jack, I knew things had gone too far. I **Jackknifed** away and **pointed** to the Awful Pawful.

Ranger Jack peered up into the tree. He whistled. Then he looked at the Jack-pack.

"I ought to put all these dogs in the pound," he said, "but there won't be room in the van with Thumper Bluey." He jerked his head toward the road.

"Everyone, take your dogs home before I change my mind. Sergeant Russell, can you give me a hand to catch that cat? Careful, now. He's worth his weight in caviar, but he's a nasty customer."

Jack's Glossary

Greet. *This is done by rising to the hind legs and clutching a person with the paws while slurping the person's face.*

Dog song. *The tuneful sound of victorious dogs.*

Jackknife. *A kind of sudden leap and twist performed by Jacks when they want to get down in a hurry.*

Point. *Jacks do this by using their noses to point to whatever they want to show you.*

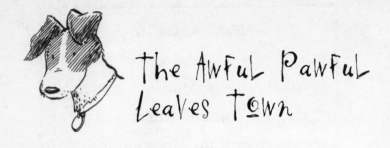

The Awful Pawful Leaves Town

The Awful Pawful left town in Ranger Jack's van.

Sarge and I watched him go. The Awful Pawful stared at me through the bars on the van. I had to speak sternly to myself. Otherwise, I might have cringed. I was afraid I hadn't seen the last of the Awful Pawful.

We went to Auntie Tidge's for supper. Auntie Tidge put iodine on Sarge and gave me a special biscuit.

"Where did the cat come from?" she asked Sarge.

"Ouch!" said Sarge. "Apparently he escaped from a freight train. Ranger Jack's been after him ever since."

"A train?" said Auntie Tidge. "What was an alley cat doing on a train?"

"Thumper Bluey is no alley cat. He's a very valuable pure breed."

"Oh dear," said Auntie Tidge. "Are Foxy Woxy and **Jackie Wackie** in trouble for treeing him?"

Sarge laughed. "I think they deserve an award for bravery, Auntie. That cat is scary, and if it wasn't for them, he'd still be on the loose."

That night, I gave my squeaker bone a thorough chewing while I reviewed the **successful conclusion** of the Case of the Awful Pawful. I didn't care that the squeaker bone didn't squeak.

11

After today I welcomed a bit of silence.

Tomorrow I'd confess to biting Lord Red on the tail.

Or pawhaps I won't bother.

Jack's Glossary

Jackie Wackie. *Auntie Tidge is the only person allowed to call me that.*

Successful conclusion. *An ending where the bleeding noses are avenged; the criminal leaves town in a van; and the detective is proud of his work.*
